2nd Edition

THIS IS GABRIEL

MAKING SENSE OF SCHOOL

A BOOK ABOUT SENSORY PROCESSING DISORDER

WRITTEN BY HARTLEY STEINER

ILLUSTRATED BY BRANDON FALL

This Is Gabriel Making Sense of School: A Book about Sensory Processing Disorder, 2nd edition

All marketing and publishing rights guaranteed to and reserved by:

721 W. Abram St.
Arlington, TX 76013
(800) 489-0727
(817) 277-2270 (fax)
e-mail: *info@sensoryworld.com*
www.sensoryworld.com

ISBN: 978-1-935567-34-9

DEDICATION

To my three sons—Gabriel, Nicholas, and Matthew—who inspire and challenge me every day.
To my parents, Stuart and Helen, for their support and unconditional love. And to Daniel, who
reminds me I have wings—and keeps me flying.

~H.S.

Dedicated to Rachelle and Tiffany, who are amazing with children,
and have chosen a career working with children with special needs.

~B.F.

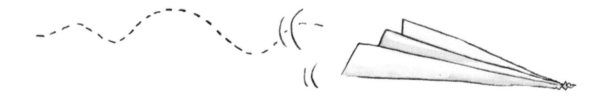

SIGHT

HEARING

TOUCH

TASTE

SMELL

VESTIBULAR

PROPRIOCEPTION

INTEROCEPTION

3

Hi, I'm Gabriel. I am good at lots of things, like riding my bike and helping people. And, I'm *super-great* at doing cannonballs! I have SPD, which stands for *Sensory Processing Disorder.* That's a big name, isn't it? It means my brain doesn't understand what my senses are telling it, which can be really hard for me—especially at school.

Did you know we have eight senses? It's true! They are sight, hearing, touch, taste, smell, proprioception, interoception, and our vestibular sense.

Those are big names! Don't worry, I'll tell you about each of them here in this book and about the things I need to make school easier on me.

Ready? Let's go!

MADE IN THE USA

5

SIGHT

Your eyes are used for sight. They help you see the world around you.

There is so much to see at school—posters, artwork, bright lights, and of course my friends and my teacher. It can be really hard to pick just one thing to look at.

It is also hard to understand what my friends are feeling by just looking at their faces. When I don't understand the look on someone's face, I might do the wrong thing, which makes me feel frustrated because I really want to have friends.

Do you know what makes it better for me?

When there isn't too much around for me to look at, then it's easier for me to focus on my teacher or my friends.

HEARING

Your ears are used to help you hear.

Noise can make me feel really overwhelmed. *Overwhelmed* is when there's too much going on and you feel a little scared and sad at the same time. I feel that way a lot in busy and crowded places, like the cafeteria—that is the worst!

Do you know what makes it better for me?

Having a quiet space—maybe under a table, or in the corner, where it isn't too loud, or wearing my headphones to block out some of the sound. Then, it's easier for me to stay calm.

TOUCH

Your fingers and skin are used for touching and to help you feel what's going on outside your body.

I don't like being touched when I don't expect it, which is really hard when I'm standing in line or sitting in a group. I also don't like scratchy clothes or itchy tags!

You know what makes it better for me?

I wear clothes that are soft on my skin. That way I can pay better attention in class! Also, it helps to hold something in my hands that feels good, like a ball of clay or a stuffed animal. Having something I like to touch makes it easier for me to focus on my work.

TASTE

Your mouth and tongue are used to help you taste.

I love almost all foods, like crunchy pretzels, creamy yogurts, and chewy fruit snacks. I also love spicy foods, like hot sauce—but not all kids with SPD like those things. Some kids just like one or two things, like chicken nuggets or macaroni and cheese.

Since I like to chew on things, sometimes I chew on my clothes or my pencil.

You know what makes it better for me?

When I have something I'm supposed to chew on, like gum or the straw in a water bottle, then it's easier for me to learn.

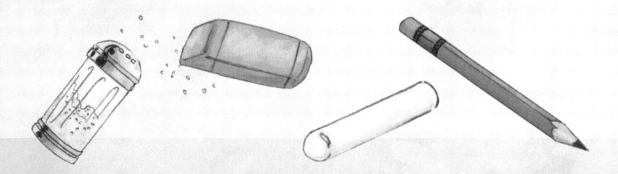

SMELL

Your nose is used to help you smell.

I don't like bad smells! Perfume, soaps, lotions, and especially certain foods smell *really gross* to me. When I smell them, all I can think about is getting away from the awful smell! But I also really like certain smells, like my mom's vanilla candle or the cinnamon she uses to make cookies.

You know what makes it better for me?

When the adults and kids around me don't wear strong-smelling perfumes, and when I can eat somewhere besides the cafeteria on days when the smells are too much.

VESTIBULAR

That's a big word! It means your sense of balance, which happens inside your ears.

I love to spin! I could spin all day long, on the playground or in a chair. I *really love* the way it feels. Some kids with SPD can be a little clumsy—they may trip over nothing at all or even fall out of their chairs. It can be hard to get the kind of movement I need to keep my body working right in the classroom.

You know what makes it better for me?

When I can get out of my chair and move around during class time. This really helps me focus when it's time to sit still.

PROPRIOCEPTION

That's an even bigger word! It means what happens inside your joints and muscles when you push and pull things. Like when you use your elbows and knees.

Pushing and pulling things is my very favorite! I love to pull the lunch wagon or hold the door open for my friends. But when I have to just sit at my desk, it feels almost impossible! If I don't get to use my joints and muscles for too long, it makes my body feel really wiggly and I just have to get up and move.

You know what makes it better?

I like to use a weighted lap pad, or squish some clay in my hands, or even help the teacher move chairs or shelve books. Doing these things helps my muscles feel really good.

19

INTEROCEPTION

That's the biggest word! It's what happens inside your body if you feel hungry or sick, or if you have to use the bathroom. Your body tells your brain what it's feeling, and where.

Sometimes I don't realize I'm hungry until I'm starving, or that I have to use the bathroom until it's an emergency! It's hard for me to understand what my body is telling me, and it can get worse when my other senses are feeling overwhelmed.

You know what makes it better?

When all of the other sensory stuff around me is not so bad, then it's easier for me to understand what my body is telling me.

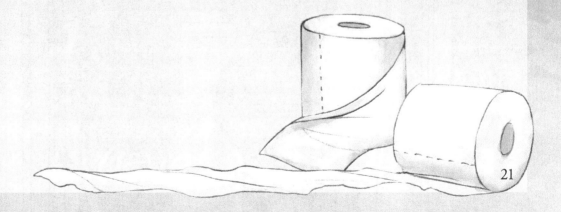

Now that we've learned about all of our eight senses and about Sensory Processing Disorder, I hope you understand why school can be hard for me. The things that make it easier for me to learn, like squishing clay, or chewing gum, or having quiet time, are really important for me to keep my body feeling calm and ready to learn.

I love school! And with a little help from my teachers and my classmates, I can be a learning sensation!

Thanks for reading!

Your friend,

Gabriel

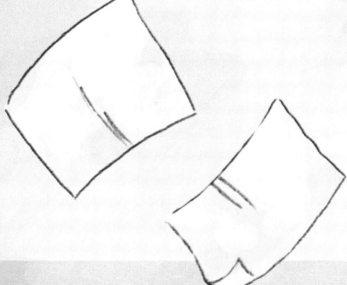

IMPORTANT INFORMATION FOR PARENTS, EDUCATORS, AND THERAPISTS:

Each year, the number of kids who receive a diagnosis of Sensory Processing Disorder continues to grow. Currently, the SPD Foundation in Denver, Colorado, estimates that as many as one in six has sensory symptoms significant enough to affect his or her social, emotional, and academic development. It is important to educate ourselves and others about how sensory differences affect millions of children.

Whether you are a parent, educator, or therapist, your help is needed to facilitate learning for kids with SPD in the classroom.

There are simple things you can do for the children in your care, like giving them sensory breaks, providing "quiet space" for them to calm down (eg, under a desk or in a quiet corner), offering options for standing up or sitting on a ball at their desks, providing a weighted lap pad and pencil grips, and offering opportunities to get proprioceptive input by doing "heavy work." For more specific ideas, contact your school's occupational therapist or your child's private occupational therapist to tailor an individualized program for your student.

FOR MORE INFORMATION ON SPD, CHECK OUT THESE RESOURCES:

SPD Foundation – *www.spdfoundation.net*
The SPD Foundation is a world leader in research, education, and advocacy for SPD, a neurological condition that disrupts the daily lives of many children and adults. Originally called the KID Foundation, the SPD Foundation provides hope and help to individuals and families living with SPD.

Hartley's Life with 3 Boys – *www.hartleysboys.com*
This is Hartley Steiner's personal blog, chronicling her life raising three boys with various diagnoses, while trying to keep her sanity and sense of humor.

SPD Blogger Network – *www.spdbloggernetwork.com*
The SPD Blogger Network is a group blog designed for those writing—or those who want to write—about raising a child with SPD. It is a place to share stories—*all* of our stories. Please join! *Sensational Chaos. Sensational Joys. Sensational Lives.*

Sensory Planet – *www.sensoryplanet.com*
The goal of Sensory Planet is to bring a positive, purposeful, and valuable social network community to those whose lives are affected by SPD. By building a network that brings all our resources together, we will greatly strengthen understanding on an individual level, as well as a community level. *Sensory Planet—One Puzzle, Many Pieces. Come explore our planet!*

ABOUT THE AUTHOR

Hartley Steiner lives in the Seattle area with her three sons. Hartley is the author of the book *Sensational Journeys*, the founder of the SPD Blogger Network *(www.spdbloggernetwork.com)*, and a contributing writer for the SPD Foundation's blog, *S.I. Focus* magazine, and *Autism Spectrum Quarterly*, among dozens of other Web sites and blogs. You can find her chronicling the never-ending chaos that is her life on her blog, Hartley's Life with 3 Boys *(www.hartleysboys.com)*, and on Twitter as @ParentingSPD. When she isn't writing or dealing with a meltdown, she enjoys spending time in the company of other adults—preferably with good food and even better wine.

ABOUT THE ILLUSTRATOR

Brandon Fall has always loved illustration, and remembers spending countless hours of his childhood getting lost in his drawings. He is now fortunate to make a living continuing to do what he loves. When he is not illustrating or designing, he enjoys spending time with his wife and children in the beautiful outdoors. You can see more of his work at *www.fallillustration.com*.

ANOTHER GREAT SENSORY WORLD TITLE BY HARTLEY STEINER

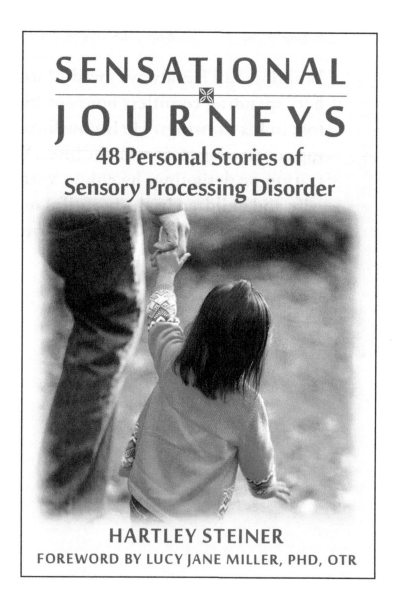

OTHER CHILDREN'S BOOKS

Michele Griffin

Jennie Harding

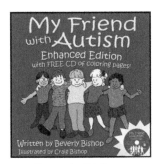
Beverly Bishop

Marla Roth-Fisch

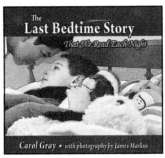
Carol Gray

Lynda Farrington Wilson

Carol Kranowitz

All of these titles and more are at www.sensoryworld.com

CPSIA information can be obtained at www.ICGtesting.com
Printed in the USA
BVOW10s0742200514

354027BV00003B/3/P